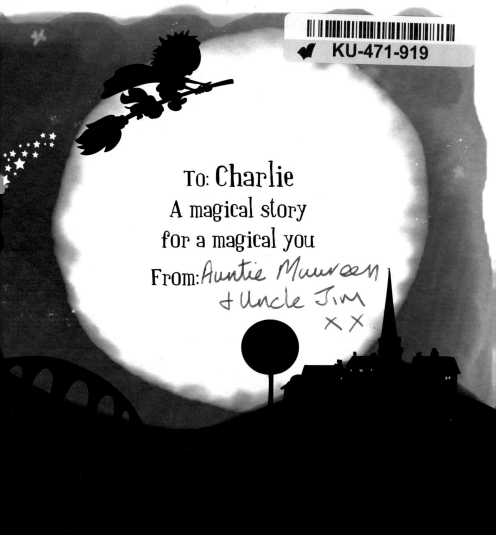

To: Charlie
A magical story
for a magical you
From: Auntie Maureen
+ Uncle Jim
x x

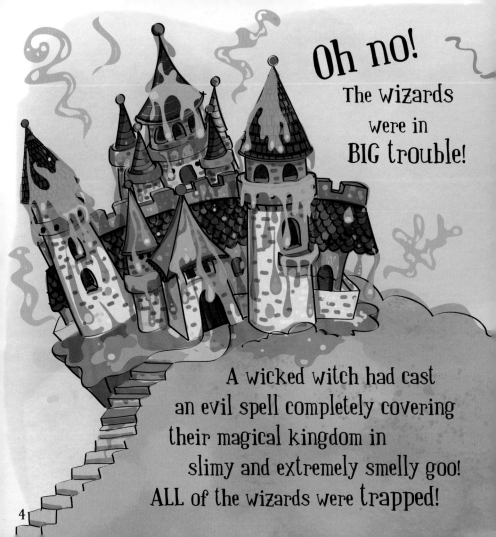

Oh no!
The wizards
were in
BIG trouble!

A wicked witch had cast
an evil spell completely covering
their magical kingdom in
slimy and extremely smelly goo!
ALL of the wizards were trapped!

4

The wizards really needed someone to help them catch the wicked witch, but **who?**

5

The wise old grand wizard looked through his special telescope, and spotted someone who might just be able to help them.

"Quickly! Send Magical Master Owl to ask for Charlie's help in saving us from the wicked witch!" shouted the wizard.

6

Magical Master Owl knew he had
to help so he flapped and fluttered
as swiftly as he could to find the boy
spotted through the telescope.

7

"WHIZZ BAM !"
Charlie said, as he waved his pretend wand towards his dog Ruffles.

"Oh Ruffles you are supposed to turn into a **flying dog.**"

Charlie SO wanted to be a Wizard.

Suddenly
with a flitter and
a flap, Magical
Master Owl
squawked through Charlie's
window into the bedroom and
explained (in his best owlish) the
trouble the wizards were in, and
asked a shocked Charlie
if he could help.

9

"Of course!"
said a delighted Charlie.

So Magical Master Owl squawked three times, flapped his wings four times, and with a WHIZZ PUFF, a broomstick, cape and magic wand suddenly appeared!

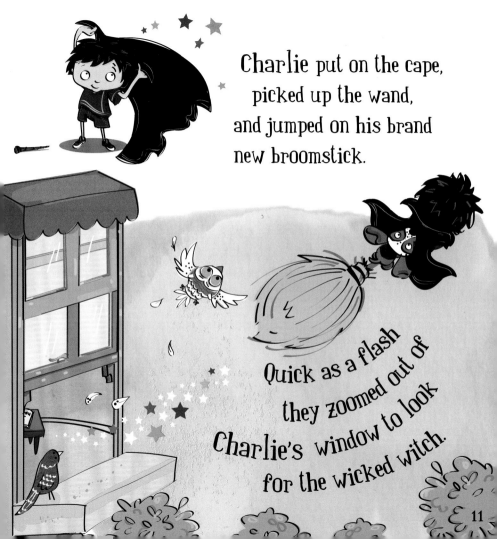

Charlie put on the cape,
picked up the wand,
and jumped on his brand
new broomstick.

Quick as a flash
they zoomed out of
Charlie's window to look
for the wicked witch.

11

The wicked witch was flying around, covering everything and everyone with her yucky, smelly green goo.

"Wahahaha!" she cackled, "Soon the whole world will be covered in my smelly goo and there are no wizards here to stop me!"

12

But little did she realise that Charlie was on his way.

He zoomed under bridges...

...and over houses, looking for the goo-spreading witch.

13

Suddenly Ruffles made
a big booming **bark**.
His super-smelling nose had caught
a whiff of the wicked witch, but she
was too far away for Charlie
to cast a spell on her.

Charlie clicked
his heels, gripped his
broomstick even tighter,
and zoomed at supersonic speed
towards the wicked witch.

15

Finally Charlie caught up with the wicked witch.

"Who are you?" the wicked witch sneered, as she launched a massive dollop of sticky green goo at Charlie.

With lightning speed
Charlie waved his magic wand.
"BIZZ POP GOO I will stop you!" he shouted.
A huge brightly-coloured umbrella appeared,
deflecting all of the smelly goo.

17

The wicked witch squealed with anger, zapping another dollop of smelly green goo towards Charlie.

"WHIZZ SPLAT send me your hat!" Charlie shouted.

The witch's hat flew off her head, catching all of her smelly green goo. Yuck!

The witch couldn't believe what this boy wizard was doing!

"ZIP ZAP, you will be
trapped in your hat!"
Charlie cast another spell.

The witch's goo-filled hat
flew back to her,
squashing down
over her head,
squishing
her in the
smelly
green goo.

Hurray the wicked witch was trapped!

A triumphant Charlie took the wicked witch back to the wizards' castle.

All the slippery, slimy green goo had now gone thanks to Charlie breaking the bad witch's horrible spell.

The wizards were so grateful to
Charlie that they let him keep the cape,
broomstick AND magic wand!

Charlie finally felt like a true wizard!

The End

COLOUR
ME IN

_____'S

BOOK OF
SPELLS